Burly Reid

By Jill Eggleton

Illustrated by Rob Kiely

Rigby

Burly Reid

When I was a kid, I lived in a town called Hika. We had a small, ordinary house with a backyard big enough for a vegetable garden and a hundred hens. The hens, of course, laid eggs – heaps of eggs. My brother and I had to collect them, clean them, and pack them in cardboard trays. We sold the eggs to people in Hika. Most of the people in Hika lived in small, ordinary houses, except for Burly Reid. He was a V.I.P. in Hika.

Clarify:
V.I.P.

A vacant in passing
B very important person
C vibrant intellectual person

A, B, or C?

...heaps of eggs

Burly Reid was big and rich – mega rich! He lived in a monstrous white mansion on the hill. He drove a gleaming silver car with a black leather roof that he slid back on hot days. And . . . Burly Reid owned a helicopter! His own private helicopter!

He was mega rich all right.

Sometimes Burly Reid strolled around the streets of Hika in his tall hat and boots with gold-studded heels that clacked like castanets. My brother said it was real gold on his boots, like the gold in his watch. "Burly Reid probably has enough gold in his watch to buy a jumbo jet," he said.

Metaphor or Simile?

... gold-studded heels that clacked like castanets

A **simile** compares one thing to another by using the words "like" or "as", and often creates a mental picture in the reader's mind.

A **metaphor** compares one thing to another without using the words "like" or "as", and often creates a mental picture in the reader's mind.

Whenever we could, we would walk past Burly Reid's house and peep through the massive iron gates, wondering what it would be like to live like him. We would make up stories about the two silent stone sentries standing guard on the marble steps and try and guess what was behind that big wooden door. Some kids said Burly Reid had a gold bathtub and a gold toilet seat!

The only person in Hika who had ever been in Burly Reid's house was Glynn Edgar's father. He was a plumber, and had been in the house to fix Burly Reid's indoor swimming pool. He said Burly Reid had a gymnasium, a home theater, a tennis court and a go-cart racetrack.

In the entire town of Hika, there were none of these things. Burly Reid had them all, right there in his house on the hill.

Question:

Why do you think not many people had been in Burly Reid's house?

One day after school, Dad said Burly Reid wanted six dozen eggs. "Six dozen eggs!" we said. Burly Reid never bought eggs from us and now he wanted six dozen.

"What does he want all those eggs for?" I asked.

"I don't know," said Dad.

"V.I.P.s use eggs for unusual things," my brother said. "They don't eat them like ordinary people do. He probably wants to put them on his go-cart track. Imagine smacking into six dozen eggs."

Awesome!

"Don't be silly," I said. "Even V.I.P.s wouldn't waste eggs like that."

"You kids can deliver the eggs," Dad said. "But make sure you wash them properly. You can't leave any dirt or feathers on the shells!"

Synonym:

A word or phrase with a meaning similar to another word.

Which words are synonyms for **awesome**?

fantastic   horrendous
amazing
wonderful   weird

We were going to deliver eggs to Burly Reid!

We were as excited as bopping baboons.

This was our chance to see inside the iron gates. This was our chance to walk on those marble steps and imagine for a moment we were V.I.P.s.

We sorted out the eggs until we had six dozen all the same size. Then we spent hours washing them. "They have to be perfect," my brother said. "It's like taking eggs to the president. You would only take perfect eggs to the president!"

I didn't think it really mattered if Burly Reid was going to put them on his go-cart track and smash them to smithereens in two seconds.

Emotions:

Which words best describe how the kids might be feeling about going to Burly Reid's house?

excited   fearful

happy   nervous

angry

We put the eggs in their cardboard trays and carried them carefully up the hill to Burly Reid's house. There was no lock on Burly Reid's gates, just a silver box with a button. We pushed the button. Burly Reid's voice squeezed out from the holes in the box.

"Can I help you?" he asked.

"We have your eggs," I said.

"Good," said the silver box. "You can leave them on the steps."

predict:
What do you think might happen in the story now?
?

... voice squeezed out

13

The massive iron gates slid open on silent wheels. Burly Reid's house loomed before us. Grand, majestic, stately.

I felt like a single ant in a giant jelly sandwich.

My brother gave me the eggs. "You can put them on the steps," he said. "I want to see the go-cart track."

Question:

Why do you think the narrator felt like a single ant in a giant jelly sandwich?

Just as I was about to put down the eggs, Burly Reid's huge Doberman dog came bounding around the corner like a bull on a rampage. It lunged at me with its long Doberman legs, licking my face with a tongue that felt like sandpaper.

I stepped back. The eggs quivered in their cardboard trays. The Doberman lunged again, licking at me like a kid licks an ice cream cone. I couldn't hold on to the eggs. They popped out of their cardboard trays and shattered on Burly Reid's marble steps. The yolks oozed out and ran like a yellow river around the feet of the silent stone sentries. My brother hadn't even gotten to the corner of the house when he heard the commotion.

... like a bull on a rampage

Action and Consequence:

ACTION	CONSEQUENCE
Burly Reid's huge Doberman dog came bounding around the corner like a bull on a rampage.	I stepped back. The eggs quivered.

Find another action and consequence . . .

We didn't stop to think. We ran like frightened ferrets.

"Thanks very much for the eggs," cackled the silver box as we screeched through the gates and down the hill.

"Burly Reid will be mad when he finds the eggs," my brother said when we got home. "We'll have to go back and apologize. Anyway, I didn't have time to see the go-cart track or the helicopter."

"I'm not going back," I said. "That Doberman's tongue will peel my skin off like a monkey peels a banana. We don't have any more eggs, anyway. Dad can take him some more tomorrow."

Inference:

What can you infer about the narrator's brother when he said, "We'll have to go back and apologize."?

.... we ran like frightened ferrets

Later that night, we heard sirens – fire engine sirens piercing the night. We leaped out of bed and looked out the window. There was a huge red glow above Burly Reid's house. Sparks were leaping and dancing and stabbing the night sky. "Burly Reid's having a fireworks party," I said. "That's why he wanted the eggs."

But he wasn't having a party. Burly Reid's house was on fire! Dad said he had to go and see what he could do to help. We gazed out the window at the fire. My brother said it was probably my fault for dropping the eggs. I said, "Don't be silly. How could me dropping eggs make Burly Reid's house catch fire?" My brother said that the Doberman could have slipped in the yolk and spun so fast along the marble steps that his claws ignited, and that's what started the fire.

20

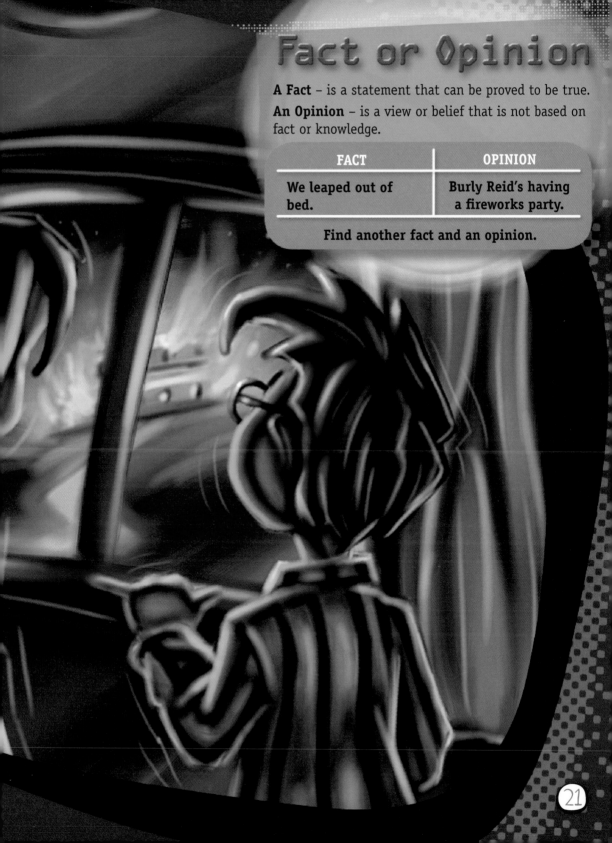

Fact or Opinion

A Fact – is a statement that can be proved to be true.

An Opinion – is a view or belief that is not based on fact or knowledge.

FACT	OPINION
We leaped out of bed.	Burly Reid's having a fireworks party.

Find another fact and an opinion.

It was hours before Dad came back. When he did, he had Burly Reid and the Doberman with him. They were all covered in black ash. "Mr. Reid is staying with us for a few days," Dad said.

Staying with us! Burly Reid, the V.I.P. of Hika! Staying with us! "He won't like staying here," I said. "We don't have a pool or tennis court. We don't have a gymnasium or home theater or a gold bathtub or gold toilet seat."

"Neither do I, now," said Burly Reid. "My house has burnt to the ground. There's nothing much left but a few black blobs of twisted metal."

We told Burly Reid we were really sorry about his house. "Well," he said, "at least I'm OK and Doberman didn't get a hair singed." Then he looked at us and winked. "And," he said, "I don't have to clean all that egg off my marble steps!"

Burly Reid stayed with us for a week. He was really cool. He had been an adventurer and a thrill-seeker. He had trekked over mountains in Greenland, traveled with nomads through the Sahara Desert, and canoed down the Amazon River. He had bungy-jumped, skydived, and driven racing cars. "Burly Reid *is* a V.I.P.," I said to my brother. "He's a very interesting person!"

A few months later, we saw Burly Reid's new house being built on the hill.

"It's going to be a mansion again," my brother said.

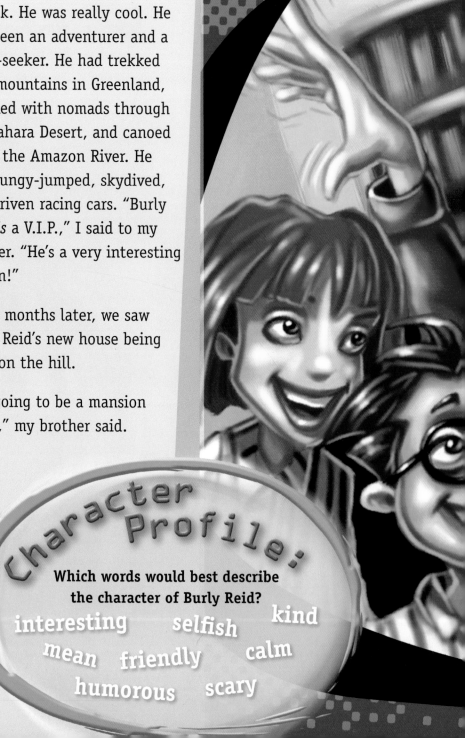

Character Profile:

Which words would best describe the character of Burly Reid?

interesting   selfish   kind

mean   friendly   calm

humorous   scary

24

And it was. It had massive iron gates. It had a big wooden door with a snake-head knocker and two silent stone sentries standing guard on the marble steps.

But . . . it didn't have a swimming pool or tennis court or go-cart racetrack.

Burly Reid gave those things to the people of Hika. "The whole town can use them," he said.

Burly Reid was a V.I.P. all right – a really cool V.I.P.!

Summary:

Which main points would you put in a summary of *Burly Reid*?

- The narrator and her brother collected and packed eggs to sell to the people in Hika.

- The narrator and her brother had to deliver eggs to Burly Reid, who lived in a monstrous white mansion on the hill.

- Burly Reid drove a gleaming silver car with a black leather roof that he slid back on hot days.

- Burly Reid opened the massive iron gates to the mansion and told the kids to leave the eggs on the steps.

- The narrator dropped the eggs on the marble steps.

- The narrator and her brother ran home.

- Burly Reid's house caught fire and Dad went to help.

- Burly Reid's house burned to the ground.

- Dad and Burly Reid were covered in black ash.

- Burly Reid and his Doberman came to stay with the narrator and her family.

- Burly Reid built a new mansion.

Think about the Text

Making connections – What connections can you make to the text?

being kind

being generous

being nervous

Text-to-Self

being inquisitive

being brave

feeling excitement

making judgements

Text-to-Text

Talk about other stories you may have read that have similar features. Compare the stories.

Text-to-World

Talk about situations in the world that might connect to elements in the story.

Planning a Personal Recount

 Think about an introduction.

Who

... when
we were
kids

When

Where

What

Think about events in order of time.

The narrator and her brother had to deliver eggs to Burly Reid, who lived in a monstrous white mansion on the hill.

→

Burly Reid opened the massive iron gates to the mansion and told the kids to leave the eggs on the steps.

The narrator was frightened by a Doberman dog, and she dropped the eggs on the marble steps.

←

The narrator and her brother ran home.

→

Burly Reid's house caught fire and Dad went to help.

Burly Reid's house burned to the ground.

→

Burly Reid and his Doberman came to stay with the narrator and her family.

Think about the conclusion.

Burly Reid built a new mansion.

In a Personal Recount ...

(a) the narrator's own responses and reactions are recorded

(b) events are recorded in a sequence, and links to time are made

(c) events all relate to one particular occasion, happening, or idea

(d) there is a conclusion at the end, that could include an interpretation of events, or a personal comment

(e) past tense is used

(f) first person is used

(g) the narrator was personally involved in the event